My Little
Red Car

My Little Red Car

Chris L. Demarest

Caroline House
Boyds Mills Press

To Laura–
who has seen the world
  –C.D.

Published by Caroline House
Boyds Mills Press, Inc.
A Highlights Company
910 Church Street
Honesdale, Pennsylvania 18431

Publisher Cataloging-in-Publication Data
Demarest, Chris L.
My little red car / written and illustrated by Chris L. Demarest.
[32]p.: col. ill.;   cm.
Summary: A boy takes an imaginary trip around the world on the
red car he gets for his birthday.
ISBN 1-878093-86-X
1. Picture books–Juvenile literature. [1. Picture books.] I. Title.
             [E]   1992
Library of Congress Catalog Card Number: 91-77597

Book designed by Joy Chu
The text of this book is set in 20-point Century Old Style.
The illustrations are done in watercolors.
Distributed by St. Martin's Press
Printed in Hong Kong

10 9 8 7 6 5 4 3 2 1

I have a wish. . .

When I grow up, I want to travel
around the world.

I'll say good-bye to my family,

then wave to all my friends.

I'll cross many streams. . .

Spiral up tall mountains. . .

Zoom down deep valleys in a flash.

I'll cross a huge river filled with
ships from all over the world.

I'll weave through many cities.

I'll zig-zag toward the ocean,

then zip along the shore like the wind.

I'll crawl through a tunnel

deep under the sea. . .

And stop for lunch

in a beautiful old city.

I'll speed over hot desert sands,

Then cool off at the North Pole.

And when it gets dark, I'll head back home. . .

Me and my little red car.